VICTORY SCHOOL SUPERSTARS

Sports Illustrated KIDS

STONE ARCH BOOKS
a capstone imprint

Sports
Illustrated
KIDS

Skating Is Hard When You're Homesick

by Julie Gassman
illustrated by Jorge Santillan

STONE ARCH BOOKS
a capstone imprint

Sports Illustrated KIDS *Skating is Hard When You're Homesick*
is published by Stone Arch Books — A Capstone Imprint
151 Good Counsel Drive, P.O. Box 669
Mankato, Minnesota 56002
www.capstonepub.com

Art Director: Bob Lentz
Graphic Designer: Hilary Wacholz
Production Specialist: Michelle Biedscheid

Timeline photo credits: Library of Congress (middle left);
Shutterstock/Gelpi (top right), Juha Sompinmäki (top left);
Sports Illustrated/Manny Millan (bottom right), Simon Bruty
(bottom left).

Printed in the United States of America in Stevens Point, Wisconsin.
009824R

Library of Congress Cataloging-in-Publication Data
Gassman, Julie. Skating is hard when you're homesick / by Julie A.
Gassman; illustrated by Jorge H. Santillan.
   p. cm. — (Sports illustrated kids. Victory School superstars)
Summary: Alicia becomes homesick while on a school trip to Triumph
Mountain, but with help of her friend, she achieves her goal in ice skating.
ISBN 978-1-4342-2237-4 (library binding)
ISBN 978-1-4342-3398-1 (pbk.)
1. School field trips—Juvenile fiction. 2. Friendship—Juvenile fiction.
3. Homesickness—Juvenile fiction. [1. Ice skating—Fiction. 2. School
field trips—Fiction. 3. Friendship—Fiction. 4. Homesickness—Fiction.]
I. Santillan, Jorge, ill. II. Title. III. Title: Skating is hard when you are
homesick.
   PZ7.G2265Sk 2012
   [Fic]—dc22   2011002308

TABLE OF CONTENTS

ALICIA GOHL

Figure Skating

AGE: 10
GRADE: 4
SUPER SPORTS ABILITY: Super jumping

VICTORY SCHOOL SUPERSTARS

Triumph Mountain Superstars:

KENZIE

ALICIA

DANNY

TRIUMPH MOUNTAIN

Triumph Mountain is the leading sports-education resort in the country. It is home to dozens of ski lifts and a state-of-the-art ice arena and snowboard park. At Triumph, young athletes can learn their favorite winter sports from their favorite athletes.

1. Ice Arena
2. Lodge
3. Condos
4. Halfpipe
5. Jumps
6. Ski Slopes

CHAPTER 1

Triumph Mountain

"Can you believe this?" I ask my friend Josh as we trudge through fresh fallen snow. "A whole week here at Triumph Mountain. No homework. No parents bugging us to make our bed or set the table. It's so great!"

"You've got that right!" Josh agrees.

Josh and I are students at the Victory School for Super Athletes. Like all the kids at our school, we have amazing sports skills.

I'm a cheerleader with a jump that reaches the sky. Josh is a super skater who lands every axel, lutz, and flip he tries. He's turned his super skating into countless wins in the hockey rink, too.

Every year, the fourth, fifth, and sixth graders at Victory go on a school trip to Triumph Mountain. We get to try different winter sports, like snowboarding, skiing, even speed skating — pretty much anything you would watch in the Winter Olympics.

"What lessons are you going to sign up for first?" asks Josh.

We've reached our destination — the resort lodge. It's time to sign up for classes for the week. But the line is long, so we'll be here a while.

"I'm not sure," I reply. "Maybe skiing. I want to try something on a mountain."

"What do you think about taking some figure skating lessons?" Josh asks.

I shake my head.

"Nah . . . I can already skate good enough that I don't fall. Plus, I can hit the rink anytime I want to back at Victory. I want to use this time to try something I can't do at home," I explain.

"Well, with your jumping, you'd be an excellent skater," Josh says. He looks like he is trying to sell me something. His grin is big, and he's practically batting his eyes.

I suddenly feel suspicious. "Why do you want me to figure skate so bad anyway?" I ask.

"I really think you'd be good. I also think you would enjoy it, but . . ." He pauses and grins at me again. "I'd also love it if you started a cheer squad for the hockey team."

A Squad for Hockey?

"What? You know I can't start a squad," I say. "That's like you starting a hockey team. The school wouldn't allow it!"

"I happen to know that my coach is going to talk to your coach about it. She's more likely to say yes if she knows that you have experience on the ice," Josh says.

"I don't know —" I start to say.

"Please," Josh begs, "I hate being one of the only teams without cheerleaders!"

I love cheerleading, especially when the teams appreciate it. And from everything Josh says, he and the rest of the guys would be grateful to have a squad in their corner.

"All right," I finally agree. "Let's see if I can get some lessons, but you're going to have to help me write some hockey cheers."

"Deal!" Josh says.

It's finally our turn. We scan the sign-up sheets.

Josh frowns and says, "Aw, man, figure skating lessons are all full for the first three days."

I'm secretly thrilled. Now I can try skiing! "That's okay. I'll take lessons the second part of the week. That way I can do downhill skiing the first part of the week."

"Yeah, that should work," Josh says. "I guess I'll sign up for . . . speed skating!"

"What? You are supposed to try something different from your regular sport. I don't think speed skating is different enough for you," I point out.

"Just kidding. How about snowboarding? Is that different enough for you?" Josh asks.

"Yes!" I say, laughing.

Homesick!

It's been three days since we arrived at Triumph Mountain. The first day was okay, but the next two days? Not so much. Something really bad happened. Something I never expected. I got homesick.

"What's wrong?" my roommate Carmen asks. She has just returned from a snowshoeing tour. I guess my red eyes are pretty noticeable.

"Nothing," I say. But then tears burst from my eyes. "I guess I miss my parents," I finally admit.

"Oh, I'm sorry," Carmen says as she puts her arm around me.

"I've never been away from them for more than one night at a time," I say.

"It will be okay," she says. "You'll see. You just need to get some rest, and then tomorrow you'll start figure skating lessons. You'll be so distracted, you won't have time to miss them."

"I guess," I say. I really hope she's right.

I go to sleep and get a lot of rest.

But ten hours later, it is clear that
Carmen was wrong. I'm supposed to be
doing waltz jumps. I launch off my front
foot and try to turn. But I'm not focused.
My jump is too big — so big that I fly half
way across the rink.

Usually, I am sure-footed as I land my jumps, but I'm not used to landing on ice. Instead of landing on my back foot like I am supposed to, my skate slides out from under me. *Whoosh!* I fall sprawled out on my front side and slide another ten feet.

Falling once wouldn't be such a big deal, but I just fell for the third time in less than two minutes. My first figure skating lesson is a total flop.

"Ugh! I can't do this," I say.

My teacher overhears me. She's Marissa Chen, two-time world figure skating champion. And even though she's super famous, she's super nice, too.

"Sure you can, Alicia," says Marissa. "I've heard all about your jumping. That is the perfect skill for figure skating."

I know she's right, but I just can't do it today. Skating is hard when you're homesick.

"I'm really sorry, Marissa, but I'm not feeling too well," I say. And when you think about it, it's true. I feel awful.

"Okay, I'll have someone walk you back to your room so you can rest. Hopefully, I'll see you back here tomorrow," she says.

"Hopefully," I say. But I doubt I'll feel any better tomorrow. After all, unless my parents suddenly appear, I don't think I'll be cured.

CHAPTER 4

Fighting with Josh

After laying around my room for a while, I decide to head to the lodge for a hot cocoa. Maybe a little chocolate and whipped cream will make me feel better.

Suddenly, I hear a voice behind me. "I thought you would still be at your skating lesson. How did it go?"

I turn around and spot Josh. I don't want to tell him that I skipped most of the lesson. "Um, not so great," I admit. "I wasn't feeling well and left after a few minutes."

"But you feel better now?" he asks with distrust.

"Sure, I mean chocolate always makes people feel better," I say. Maybe if I make a joke, he'll quit asking me questions.

"You know, Alicia, if you didn't want to cheer for hockey, you should have just said so before I got my hopes up," says Josh.

"What?" I say. "I didn't say that!" I can feel tears forming again. I don't want to cry, but I miss my parents so much. And now Josh is practically yelling at me.

"You didn't have to. I know you aren't sick. You just skipped," he says.

I can't hold my tears any longer. They spill down my face. "I'm really sorry, Josh," I say. "I just haven't been feeling like myself. I want to go home!"

I can tell he feels embarrassed about seeing me cry. He might even think it's his fault, but it isn't. "Jeez, Alicia, please don't cry. I'm sorry," he says.

"The truth is, Josh, my lesson went terrible. I kept falling — hard. I can't focus. I miss my mom and dad so much. It stinks!" I say.

"You're homesick?" Josh asks. "But that isn't like you. You're tough. You proved that cheerleading was a real sport to the whole football team. Nothing bothers you."

"Yeah, well, it turns out that being away from home for more than a day or two bothers me," I say, embarrassed.

"And then I go and yell at you," Josh says, shaking his head. "I'm sorry."

"It's okay. Maybe I should tell one of the chaperones. Maybe my mom or dad could come and get me early," I say.

"No, not yet. I have an idea. Give me two hours and meet me at the rink," Josh says excitedly. "If you still feel lousy afterward, I'll go with you to talk to a chaperone."

I don't say anything at first. But when I notice the excitement on his face, I can't say no. "All right, I'll see you in two hours."

My Own Cheerleaders

I can't believe what I'm seeing. Five of my friends, including my twin brother, Danny, are all in skates on the ice. There's Carmen, Kenzie, Tyler, and, of course, Josh.

When they see me, they all skate into a line and grin. They start yelling together.

You're number one.

Camp is fun.

Don't be homesick.

Just watch this trick.

Suddenly, Josh speeds off. He launches
into a series of jumps. I see a double lutz,
followed by a double salchow. After his
backward landing, he settles into a sit spin.
He's practically a blur, he's moving so fast.

I can't help but laugh. "Nice cheer guys," I say. "And Josh, you are awesome."

"I didn't know you were feeling homesick, sis," says Danny. "Are you feeling any better?"

Am I? I ask myself. "Yeah! I think I am," I say finally. "It's hard to feel bad with great friends like you. Thanks everyone. I mean it."

"Good," says Josh, "because we have a lot of work to do."

"We do?" I ask.

"Yep, I'm going to get you up to speed for your lesson with Marissa tomorrow," Josh replies, as he throws himself into a relaxed toe jump.

"Well, hopefully someone has my skates!" I say.

CHAPTER 6

Our Big Debut

"Here we go! Get a goal! Here we go! Get a goal!" I shout together with the rest of the brand new hockey cheer team. It is our big debut.

At the end of the period, we skate out onto the ice for our routine. I've practiced a lot since I got home from Triumph Mountain, and I can do a perfect axel.

Of course, the jumping part never caused me any problems. It was the landing that gave me some trouble.

But as I complete my twirls and turns, I know that I won't have any problems with my jumps. That's the great thing about practice. It almost always works.

The rest of the team is chanting, "Go big red and blue! Go big red and blue!"

Meanwhile I skate around them to gain speed. Finally, I launch into my jump from one foot. I spin one and a half times and land on the other foot. The crowd roars.

As we skate off the ice at the end of the performance, I catch Josh's eye as the hockey team comes back on the ice to warm up for the next period. He gives me a big thumbs-up. "Nice work!" he yells.

"Thanks!" I shout. I can't stop grinning. I started skating to help out a friend. In the end, he helped me more. That's what it's like to be a Superstar. We always look out for each other and make sure we all do our best.

GLOSSARY

appreciate (uh-PREE-shee-ate)—to enjoy or value

axel (AK-suhl)—a jump in which the skater skates forward, turns one and a half times in the air, and then lands and skates backward

chaperones (SHAP-uh-rohns)—adults who are responsible for the safety of young people at events

destination (dess-tuh-NAY-shuhn)—the place that a person or vehicle is traveling

embarrassed (em-BA-rhussed)—feeling awkward or uncomfortable

experience (ek-SPIHR-ee-uhnss)—the skill gained from doing something

lutz (LUTZ)—a jump in which a skater glides backward in a wide curve and uses the toe of the skate to launch and rotate in the opposite direction

Olympics (oh-LIM-picks)—a sports competition held every four years for athletes from all over the world

routine (roo-TEEN)—a performance that is carefully worked out so it can be repeated often

JULIE GASSMAN

The youngest in a family of nine children, Julie Gassman grew up in Howard, South Dakota. After college, she spent a winter season living and working at a ski resort in Colorado. She used her memories of the resort to write about Triumph Mountain, which she calls a snow-lover's dream destination. She now lives in southern Minnesota with her husband and their three children. Julie has written two other books about Alicia, *Cheerleading Really Is a Sport* and *You Can't Spike Your Serves*.

JORGE SANTILLAN

Jorge Santillan got his start illustrating in the children's sections of local newspapers. He opened his own illustration studio in 2005. His creative team specializes in books, comics, and children's magazines. Jorge lives in Mendoza, Argentina, with his wife, Bety; son, Luca; and their four dogs, Fito, Caro, Angie, and Sammy.

FIGURE SKATING IN HISTORY

3000 B.C. — Skating is believed to have originated in **Finland**.

1850s A.C. — Skating becomes very popular in England and North America. Skaters try jumps and spins.

1858 — The first man-made lake for public ice skating opens in **Central Park**, New York City.

1892 — The International Skating Union is formed in the Netherlands.

1896 — The first World Figure Skating Championships are held in St. Petersburg, **Russia**.

1964 — Peggy Fleming wins her first of five U.S. Women's Figure Skating Championships at age 15.

1981 — **Scott Hamilton** wins the first of four World Figure Skating Championships. In 1984, Hamilton wins Olympic gold.

1986 — Debi Thomas becomes the first African American to win the U.S. Figure Skating Championship.

1997 — At age 14, Tara Lipinski becomes the youngest U.S. figure skating champion in history.

2005 — **Michelle Kwan** wins her ninth and final U.S. Figure Skating Championship. She also holds five world championship titles.

Give A Cheer for Alicia Gohl!

If you liked reading Alicia's adventure on ice, check out her other *sports stories.*

Cheerleading Really is a Sport

Alicia's brother, Danny, and his friends are always putting down cheerleading. But Alicia knows that everyone on the team is a star athlete with a super skill. She just has to prove it to Danny.

You Can't Spike Your Serves

Alicia is organizing a volleyball tournament to raise money for her friend's cheerleading team. She is excited to play herself, but she can't seem to get her serves right. Will Alicia remember that you can't spike your serves?

STONE ARCH BOOKS
a capstone imprint